FOR MY JOY, TED —Y.I.
FOR LITTLE B.I.T. —J.D.

First U.S. edition 2020

Library of Congress Catalog Card Number pending
ISBN 978-1-5362-0934-1

20 21 22 23 24 25 CCP 10 9 8 7 6 5 4 3 2 1

Printed in Shenzhen, Guangdong, China

This book was typeset in Agenda and JenniDesmond.
The illustrations were done in mixed media.

Candlewick Press
99 Dover Street
Somerville, Massachusetts 02144

visit us at www.candlewick.com

JOY

YASMEEN ISMAIL

illustrated by JENNI DESMOND

CANDLEWICK PRESS

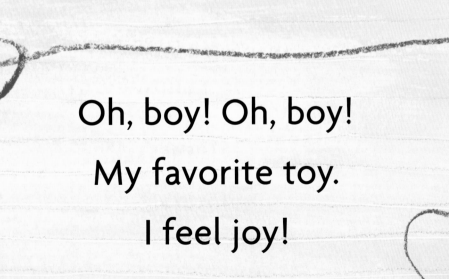

Oh, boy! Oh, boy!
My favorite toy.
I feel joy!

Jingle
jangle,

wriggle
wrangle,

in

a

tangle.

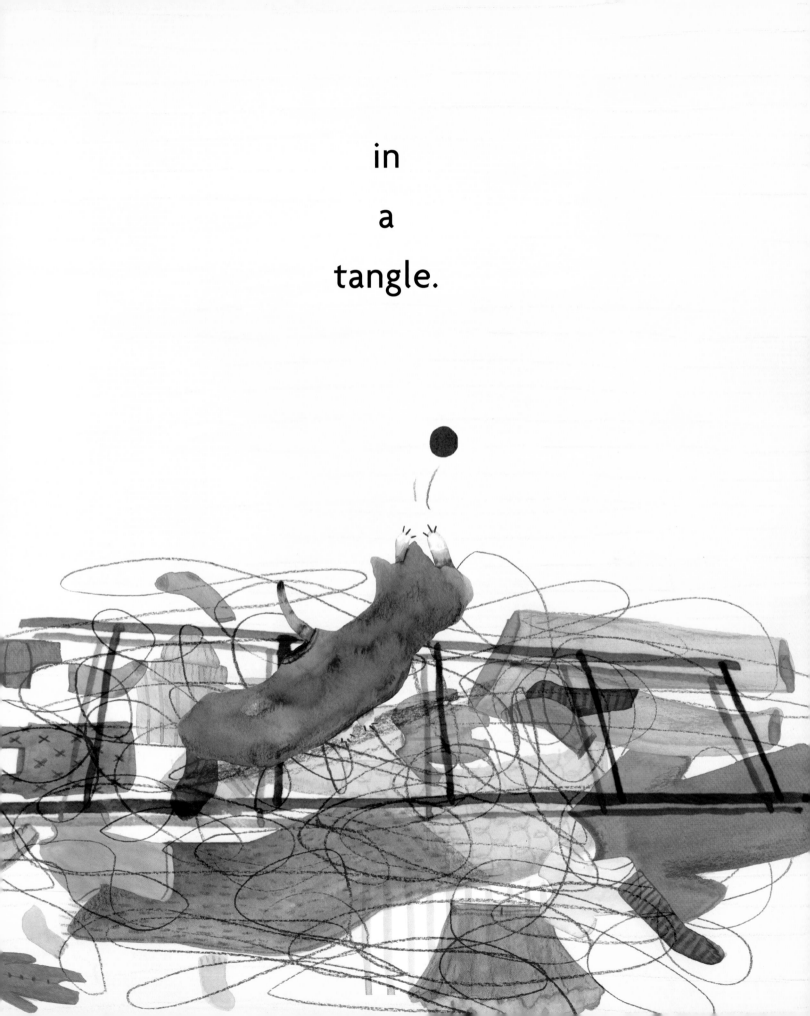

BOUNCE BOUNCE BOING BOING

Shake,
rattle,
and

ROLL,

this happy soul!

Tickle, tickle,
in a pickle.

Run, run, fun, fun.

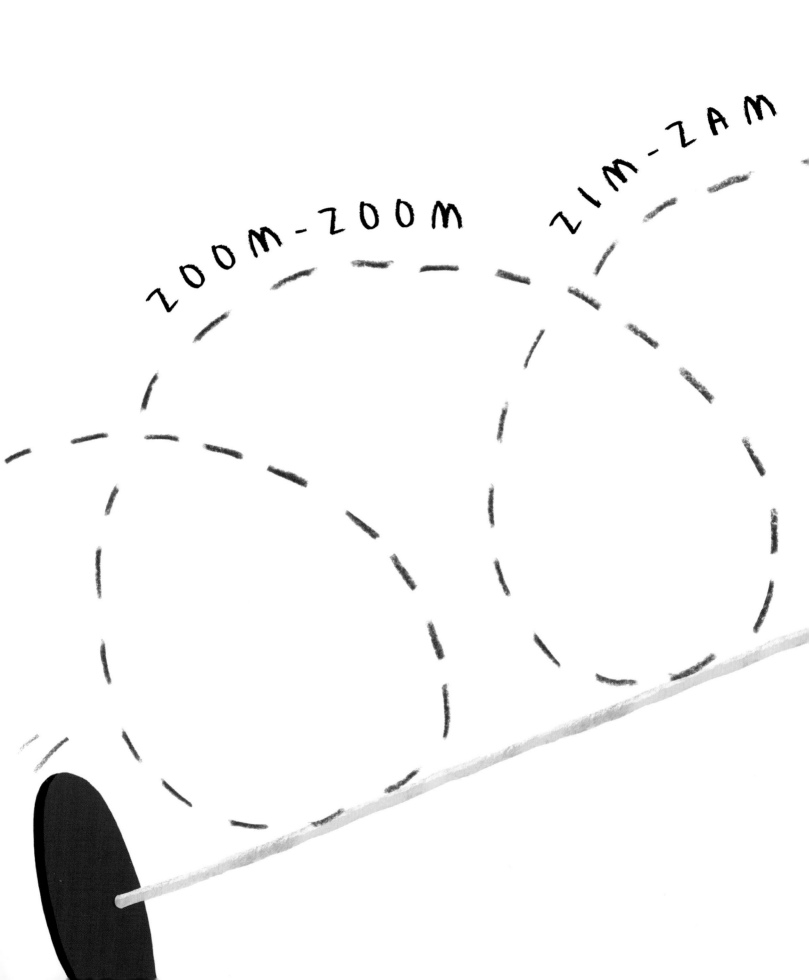

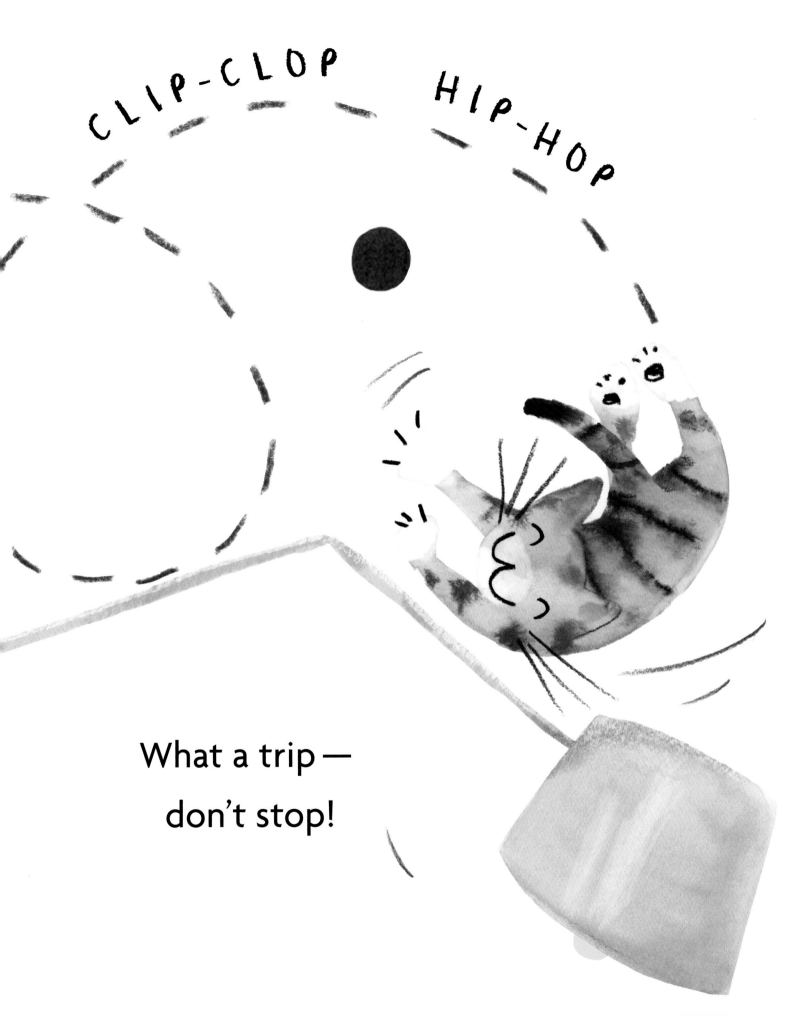

CLIP-CLOP   HIP-HOP

What a trip—
don't stop!

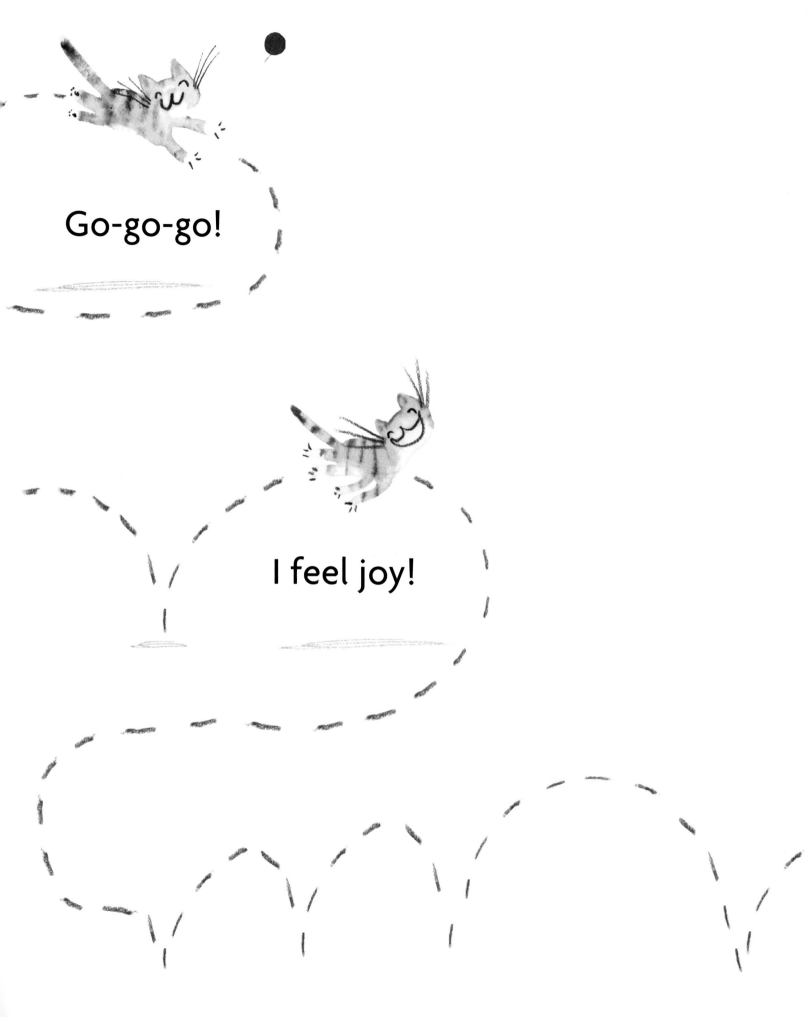

Go-go-go!

I feel joy!

UH-OH.

DONK   Ow.

Oh . . .
This is bad.
I feel sad.

Where's my mom?
Where's my dad?

A little hug, a kiss, a squeeze.
Let's check your paws
and clean your knees.

I think you're going to be just fine.
Give yourself a little time.

Now, look at me. Are you all right?
Did you get a little fright?

I'm always here if you fall.

All you have to do is call.

There's nowhere that
I'd rather be
than holding you
so close to me.

Oh, boy!

Oh, boy!

My favorite toy.

I feel joy!